ECHO and N...
A Greek and R...

by Jeannette Sanderson
illustrated by Jose Ramos

Table of Contents

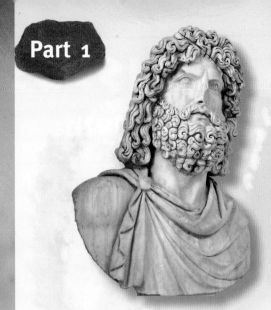

Jupiter needed to get away from his home on Mount Olympus. Being the all-powerful king of the gods was a big responsibility. So he decided to take a break and visit a lake that was home to wood **nymphs**. These spirits of nature were beautiful, playful young women. When Jupiter arrived, a dozen nymphs went to greet him.

In Greek and Roman myths, **nymphs** were minor goddesses. They lived in mountains, forests, and bodies of water.

"Let's play!" Jupiter commanded. The king of the gods smiled broadly, jumped into a fast-moving river, and the nymphs followed. Jupiter and the nymphs splashed in the waterfalls, ran in the grass, and frolicked in the woods. Jupiter was having so much fun that he forgot all about his wife, Juno, the goddess of marriage and the home.

Juno was also a very powerful goddess—and very jealous. She knew that Jupiter went to the lake to spend time with the pretty wood nymphs. Although Jupiter **denied** it, Juno knew he was lying; she just never could catch him in the lie.

Jupiter was chasing one of the nymphs around a tree when suddenly he felt a cold wind, and he stopped in his tracks almost as suddenly. The nymph nearly crashed into him.

"Thunder!" he bellowed. "I forgot to keep a lookout for Juno. I can feel that she's on her way." He took a quick look around him. His eyes settled on Echo, the most talkative of the lovely nymphs.

"Echo," Jupiter commanded. "You are good with words. Talk with Juno when she arrives. Tell her a story, tell her anything. I need time to get back to Mount Olympus before she does."

Then Jupiter disappeared. The other nymphs hid behind the trees. Echo felt a cold wind behind her. She turned around and in front of her was stormy-faced Juno!

"My queen," said Echo, bowing down. "Welcome to our lake."

Juno did not answer. She was looking over Echo's head, looking at the place where Jupiter had just stood. Echo turned to look, too. She had to think quickly.

"Isn't that a **majestic** tree, Juno!" Echo said. "Did you know it is the biggest tree in the woods? It takes six nymphs holding hands to reach all the way around it. Have you never seen that tree before?"

"I am not looking for a tree," Juno said angrily. "I am looking for my husband."

Playful Echo could not help herself and said, "Unless Jupiter has turned into a tree, he is not there."

Juno gave Echo a hard, squinty-eyed look and then roared, "I heard voices coming from this side of the mountain. Where are the other nymphs? I heard much talking."

Echo smiled nervously. "You know I like to talk, Juno. Even when I am alone, I do not stop talking."

At first, Juno did not seem **convinced**, but then she let out a long sigh. "Perhaps I just imagined it. Jupiter is such a **flirt** that I always think the worst."

Echo opened her mouth to reply, but Juno disappeared before she could speak a word. "Good-bye," Echo said. As soon as Juno was gone, the other wood nymphs came out from hiding.

"I am glad she didn't catch us!" said one nymph. "I love when Jupiter visits us!"

"Yes, oh yes," they all agreed.

flirt someone whose actions reflect an interest in another

"We had so much fun with him today running, laughing, and swimming. I hope Jupiter comes again soon," said Echo. Just then the other nymphs grew very quiet. They all seemed to be looking behind Echo, not at her. Echo sensed a problem and took a deep breath before she turned around.

"Juno!" Echo's eyes were wide as chariot wheels. "I thought you had gone."

The goddess's face was white with anger. "You lied to me!"

"I . . . I . . . was just doing as Jupiter wished," Echo said.

"Silence!" the goddess shouted. "You will be punished. Your tongue, so freely **wagged** at my expense, shall be of little use. From now on you will no longer be able to speak on your own. You will only be able to repeat the words of others."

Echo opened her mouth to speak. She wanted to explain herself, but all that came out were Juno's words. "Words of others," Echo said.

"Yes," said Juno with a mean smile. "That is your punishment."

8

wagged moved back and forth quickly

"Punishment," said Echo, her voice trailing off. "Punishment." From that day on, Echo could only repeat the words of others.

Part 2

Echo quietly went about her life in the woods. The young nymph spent most of her time alone. Then one day Echo saw a young man hunting deer. This young man was more beautiful than any she had ever seen, and Echo fell instantly in love. She wished she could say something, but she had been **cursed**, unable to speak first. All Echo could do was secretly follow the handsome young man.

The handsome young man was Narcissus, son of the river god Cephisus. His mother was a river nymph named Liriope. When Narcissus was born, Liriope went to visit blind old Tiresias the most famous **seer** of his time. It was believed he could see the future.

"My son is so beautiful," said Liriope. "I worry about him. Tell me, great seer, will Narcissus have a long life?"

seer one who can see into, and tell, the future

Like most seers, Tiresias answered in a riddle. "If he never knows himself, he will have a long life." The seer did not explain what it meant to know oneself. Liriope was still left wondering how long her son's life would be.

The baby Narcissus grew more beautiful every day. By the time he was sixteen, he had hundreds of admirers; nearly all who saw Narcissus fell in love with him. But Narcissus did not love anyone back, because he thought that he was better than everyone.

When Echo spied Narcissus in the woods, she did not know the beautiful young man had a closed heart. Echo only saw his outward beauty. Narcissus's hair was as golden as **Apollo's** sun. His eyes were as blue as **Neptune's** oceans. His cheeks were as red as **Pomona's** apples. Echo moved closer to Narcissus. As she did so, a twig snapped under her feet.

Narcissus heard the sound and stopped walking. "Is someone here?" he asked.

"Here, here," Echo answered.

"Where are you hiding?"

"Hiding, hiding," Echo said.

Narcissus looked around him. He could not see anyone, but was not surprised. Love-struck admirers often followed him. Narcissus let out a tired sigh and said, "Please, let us meet."

"Let us meet," Echo repeated.

"Yes," said Narcissus. "Come to me."

Apollo the Greek and Roman god of the sun, light, music, and healing
Neptune the Roman god of the seas
14 **Pomona** the Roman goddess of fruit trees

Echo heard Narcissus's words, but she did not hear the **annoyed** tone in the young man's voice and so she stepped sprightly from behind a tree. "Come to me," said Echo, hopefully repeating Narcissus's last words. Then the lovely nymph ran happily to Narcissus. He stepped back when he saw that it was yet another love-struck nymph. Echo did not notice the **cruelty** in Narcissus's blue eyes; she only saw the sky on a cloudless day in May. Echo reached out to touch Narcissus's cheek, but he brushed away her hand.

"Don't!" said Narcissus, backing away. "I would rather be alone than be near you."

"Near you," said Echo, reaching out her arms to be near him. "Near you."

"Go away! I could never love you," declared Narcissus as he pushed Echo away. Then he ran off.

"Love you," Echo said, tears rolling down her soft cheeks. "Love you. Love you."

Narcissus didn't hear. He had run far away.

Echo now felt colder than the moon. She found a cave and crawled inside. There she died of a broken heart. All that remained of the lovely nymph was her voice.

Part 3

Jupiter saw what happened to Echo. He remembered how Echo had tried to protect him from Juno's anger. Jupiter called for Nemesis, the goddess of **revenge**.

"Narcissus breaks hearts as if he has the power of a great god," Jupiter said. "I want you to find a way to punish this young man."

Nemesis smiled and said, "I know just the punishment. This boy shall fall in love, but it will be a love that cannot be returned."

"Take care of it," Jupiter said, and Nemesis immediately went down to the humans.

Later that day, Narcissus was again hunting in the woods when he came upon a hidden pond. With no breeze, the pond's silvery surface was smooth as glass. Narcissus grew hot and thirsty. He put down his bow and arrows and leaned over the pond. What he saw in the mirror-like water made him forget his thirst instantly. What he saw was his own **reflection**, which he'd never seen before. But Narcissus didn't know he was looking at himself; he thought he was looking at a beautiful water spirit.

revenge an action made in order to get even, or get back at someone, for a deed that was done
reflection an image seen as in a mirror

"Your face is a sunrise and your eyes are shining stars," Narcissus said to his reflection. Then he smiled hopefully at the image—and it smiled back.

"Come closer to me," Narcissus said joyfully. He leaned closer to the water. The image got closer. For the first time in his life, Narcissus felt his heart open up and fill with love.

"Let me hold you!" cried Narcissus as he reached out to touch the image. But all he touched was water. The image disappeared, yet it came back a few moments later.

"Let me kiss you!" cried Narcissus. He leaned down to kiss the image, but his lips only touched water. The image disappeared briefly, then came back.

"Everyone loves me," said a **confused** Narcissus. "Surely you must love me, too. Yet you go away when I try to touch you. Why?" Narcissus started to cry. Teardrops fell on the water and his image disappeared again into **ripples**.

"Stay!" Narcissus begged. The image returned once the water became still. "Even if I cannot touch you, at least let me look upon your beauty." Narcissus stared longingly at the water. He had fallen in love with his own reflection!

Day after day, Narcissus stared and stared at his reflection. He did not move, nor did he eat or drink. The wood nymphs who loved Narcissus tried to save him. They brought him berries and other fruits from the woods, but Narcissus refused the food. He would not even look at the nymphs. He could not take his eyes off his own image.

The once-beautiful young man began to waste away. Before long he was skin and bones. As the seer had **predicted**, Narcissus had gotten "to know himself," and it was killing him. Death was near. Narcissus forced his eyes open one last time. He looked at his reflection.

"Good-bye, my love," he whispered.

Echo's voice, all that survived of her, called back to him. "Good-bye, my love!"

Then Narcissus died of a broken heart, just as Echo had.

The nymphs heard Narcissus's final cry. They went to get his body for a funeral, but there was no body. On the spot where Narcissus had lain for many days and nights grew a flower. It had white petals and a yellow center. That flower is called narcissus.

Echo and Narcissus died long ago. But something of them still remains. Speak when you are in the mountains. You will hear Echo's voice repeat your words. And look for the beauty of Narcissus in his white and yellow flower.

GLOSSARY

annoyed   (uh-NOYD) *adjective* was showing slight anger (page 16)

confused   (kun-FYOOZD) *adjective* unable to understand (page 20)

convinced   (kun-VINST) *adjective* sure about something (page 7)

cruelty   (KROOL-tee) *noun* desire to cause other to suffer (page 16)

cursed   (KER-sed) *adjective* affected by a curse that causes something bad (page 10)

denied   (dih-NIDE) *verb* said that something was not true (page 3)

majestic   (muh-JES-tik) *adjective* large and impressively beautiful (page 5)

predicted   (prih-DIK-ted) *verb* to have said that something will happen (page 21)

ripples   (RIH-pulz) *noun* small waves on the surface of a liquid (page 20)

Questions for Close Reading

Use facts and details from the text to support your answers to the following questions.

- In Part 1, the all-powerful Jupiter tells Echo to lie for him so he won't get in trouble. In Part 3, he asks Nemesis to punish Narcissus, instead of punishing Narcissus himself. What do these actions tell you about Jupiter?

- The central theme of the myth is pride and the trouble it can cause. What details from the story support this theme?

- Tiresias is a blind seer. Seers tell what will happen in the future. Why is it important in this story that Tiresias is blind?

- What words in Part 2 helped you determine the meaning of the word *admirers*?

- Do you think Narcissus learned his lesson, or did he die still thinking he was the most beautiful thing ever made?

Comprehension: Compare and Contrast

Complete the chart and then answer the question below.

	Who did the punishing?	What was the punishment?	Why was this punishment chosen?	How did the punishment affect each character?
Echo				
Narcissus				

- What do the punishments tell you about how the gods chose punishments?